RUBY

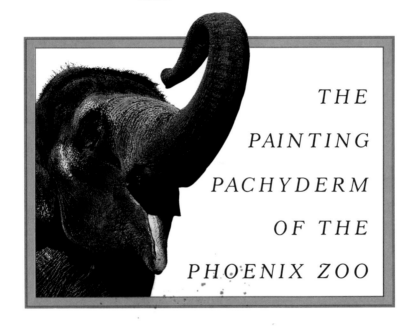

THE

PAINTING

PACHYDERM

OF THE

PHOENIX ZOO

DICK GEORGE

Delacorte Press

Published by
Delacorte Press
Bantam Doubleday Dell Publishing Group, Inc.
1540 Broadway
New York, New York 10036

Library of Congress Cataloging-in-Publication Data
George, Dick.
Ruby: the painting pachyderm of the Phoenix Zoo/by Dick George.
p.   cm.
ISBN 0-385-32100-7 (lib. bdg.)
1. Ruby (Elephant)—Juvenile literature. 2. Asiatic elephant—
Juvenile literature. 3. Animals as artists—Juvenile literature.
[1. Ruby (Elephant) 2. Elephants. 3. Phoenix Zoo (Ariz.)
4. Animals as artists.] I. Title.
QL737.P98G46   1995
636'.961—dc20   94-30626
                                                           CIP
                                                            AC

Manufactured in the United States of America
June 1995
10   9   8   7   6   5   4   3   2   1

To elephants and the other wildlife on this planet
in hopes we humans will eventually learn to be good neighbors—
to you as well as to ourselves.

And to Susan, who deserves this first one—and much more.

The artist at work.

INTRODUCTION

It's been a good morning for the elephants at the Phoenix Zoo. Ruby, an Asian elephant, and Kinte and Kewana, two African elephants, have done their morning exercises well. They've had their showers in the barn, then gone outside and thrown fresh dust on their backs. Finally, they've had breakfast: a bucket of carrots and half a bucket of munchy hay pellets apiece.

It's been a good day for the keepers too. They've cleaned up the yard and checked over the elephants. All three are healthy, happy, clean, and well fed.

Things have gone well at all the seven exhibits the keepers are responsible for. The elephants are the last. Now everyone is a little ahead of schedule and has a few minutes of free time.

It's an ideal time for Ruby to do a painting.

Keeper Tawny Carlson asks, "Ruby, do you want to paint?"

Instantly Ruby shows all the signs of excitement in an Asian elephant. Her ears flare out and she flaps them. Then she lets out a tiny, high-pitched squeak.

Keepers Jerry Brown and Anita Schanberger emerge from the barn with Ruby's paint-streaked easel, a fresh canvas, artist's paintbrushes, a palette with nine plastic jars of paint, and a coffee can full of water for cleaning the brushes.

Ruby kinks her tail and squeaks again while Jerry sets up the easel.

"Okay, Rube," says Tawny as she holds the palette. "Pick a color!"

Ruby eyes the palette for a few seconds, then touches one of the plastic jars with the tip of her trunk.

"Turquoise!" says Tawny and pops the lid off the jar of nontoxic paint.

"Pick a brush," says Anita, holding five brushes out in a fan.

Ruby ponders this choice, too, for a few seconds, then reaches out and picks a small brush.

"Give me the brush," says Tawny.

Ruby gives the brush to Tawny, who dips it into the turquoise paint and returns it. Ruby dabs the brush on the side of her trunk, then makes several diagonal strokes across the canvas.

"Need some more paint?" Tawny asks.

Ruby passes the brush back to Tawny, who dips it in the turquoise again.

Ruby makes a few more diagonal strokes, then one last vertical stroke.

"Through with that color?" Tawny asks.

Ruby is busy painting one of the wing nuts on the easel.

Tawny tries again. "Want another color?"

Ruby passes the brush to Anita to clean.

"Pick a color," Tawny says.

Again Ruby snakes up her trunk and touches a jar of paint, this time yellow.

"Pick a brush," says Anita, and Ruby pulls an inch-and-a-half-wide brush from her hand.

Ruby picks a color.

Tawny dips the big brush in the yellow paint and hands it to Ruby.

Ruby makes curves and swirls on the canvas, big bold strokes that go from edge to edge.

Her next choices are red and purple, both favorite colors.

"That's bee-YOU-tee-ful!" the keepers croon as the layers of color build on the canvas.

In different spots on the canvas, reds and yellows blend with purple and turquoise to make a muddy brown.

"That's UGH-lee!" the keepers sing out.

Her head tilted back in pleasure and her trunk arched toward the canvas, Ruby continues to paint, soaking up the keepers' affectionate words.

A few minutes later, Ruby curls her trunk and holds the brush high over her head. Then she takes two steps back from the canvas. The painting is nearly finished.

Anita takes the brush and sticks it in the can of water.

Jerry removes the canvas from the easel and holds it firmly for the finishing touch.

Tawny takes a large felt-tipped pen from her pocket, removes its cap, and hands it to Ruby.

Ruby takes the pen and makes a last few delicate strokes in the lower right-hand corner of the canvas.

"Good girl!" says Jerry as he holds the finished canvas up for Ruby to see.

"That's so PRETTY!" say Tawny and Anita.

In her enormous head, Ruby's incongruously small brown eye studies what she has just made.

Sometimes Ruby's trunk is as colorful as the canvas.

Ruby reaches out for friendship from her first home in the Children's Zoo.

1

Ruby did not always live at the Phoenix Zoo. She was born somewhere in Thailand in July 1973. No one knows exactly when or where—or even who her parents were. Most likely her father was a wild elephant living in the rain forest and her mother was a trained elephant that worked in a logging camp.

In February 1974, when she was seven months old, Ruby came to the United States. She flew in a heavy wooden crate only a little larger than she was. Together, the baby elephant and the crate weighed 360 pounds. At the airport in Phoenix, she was met by two men who lifted her crate into a small pickup. On the ride through the city, the turns and stops in traffic made it hard for her to stand steadily. She must have been relieved when she finally reached her new home, the Phoenix Zoo.

Even though it was after hours, the zoo veterinarian and several keepers were eagerly awaiting her arrival. Among them were animal trainer Paul Fritz and his wife and assistant, Joanne Fritz. The keepers lifted the crate from the truck and unlatched the door. When they opened it, the late-afternoon sunlight streamed inside and made the baby elephant blink.

"Who are these people?" she seemed to be wondering.

At first sight of the young elephant, Joanne cried, "Oh, my gosh! She's beautiful! She's a perfect little jewel. Let's name her Ruby!"

The others laughed at first, but no one had a better name—so Ruby it was.

Paul filled a stall in the barn with hay so that Ruby would be warm and dry. That night, he and Joanne slept in the hay with Ruby, feeding her and reassuring her.

In the days and weeks that followed, Ruby settled in. The Children's Zoo keepers took care of her, but Paul and Joanne came by often to visit. She stayed in the barn for a few months until the weather warmed up. Then she moved to a nearby corral that had a small barn.

That summer, Paul and Joanne worked with Ruby as part of the trained animal shows the zoo presented in those years. Ruby was much too young to learn complicated things. She was barely a year old and didn't yet have control over her trunk, which was then less than a foot long.

The elephant's trunk is an extremely complex organ. It has more than fifty thousand muscles and tendons. Like a small child learning to use its hands, an elephant is about two years old before it begins to learn to control its trunk. Most of the time, a baby's trunk just hangs limp. Sometimes, it gets in the way. A calf might even trip over its own trunk. When Joanne gave Ruby a bottle, she had to lift Ruby's trunk away from her mouth.

Onstage Ruby stole the show simply by walking on and standing there. She came on at the end of the performance and stunned everyone just by being what she was—a beautiful, tiny elephant.

At the end of the summer, the shows ended and Ruby returned to her little corral. That fall, Paul and Joanne Fritz left the zoo to start an animal sanctuary of their own.

2

After Joanne and Paul Fritz left, several keepers took turns taking care of Ruby. They fed her, cleaned up after her, and spent a few minutes each day with her. But they were busy and couldn't put in much time with Ruby because they had many other animals to care for. So Ruby didn't get as much personal attention as a young, growing elephant needs.

In the wild a baby elephant gets constant, gentle attention from its mother and the other members of the herd. Older elephants help guide, protect, and teach the younger ones. There is much to learn! Elephants depend on experience shared from one animal to another and from one generation to the next. In infancy, a calf learns the basics—how to find and eat solid food, how to get along with the others in the herd, and how to avoid danger. Most of this it learns by watching its family and friends.

But Ruby was all by herself. As you might expect, before long she began to develop some bad habits. It wasn't that Ruby was bad. She just didn't have older, wiser elephants to learn from—and the keepers didn't know how to be elephant mothers and elephant aunts.

When Ruby was little, for example, she enjoyed pushing and shoving games with her keepers. However, she quickly grew much bigger and stronger than her keepers. By the time she was two, she weighed almost seven hundred pounds. The pushing games became chasing games as the keepers ran out of the exhibit to avoid getting hurt. It was a very dangerous way to play. Someone could have been killed.

Ruby did something else alarming. She learned that if she scattered her grain around the exhibit, ducks would come in to eat. Ruby then would chase them and swat at them with her trunk. Every now and then she would hit or even kill one. Something had to be done.

Fortunately, help was on the way.

Joanie Stinson had gotten her first job at the zoo in 1974 during her junior year of high school. She sold tickets at the front gate. The next year she graduated and went to work full-time taking care of birds. Six months later, she transferred to working with large mammals, including Ruby.

Joanie's first encounter with Ruby didn't go well.

"Okay, Ruby. It's you and me," Joanie said and entered the corral.

As soon as she did, Ruby and all her seven hundred pounds came running at Joanie.

Fortunately, there was a heavy steel hayrack fastened to the side of the barn about four feet off the ground. Joanie jumped into it and stayed there, out of reach. Before long, Ruby grew tired of waiting for this new keeper to climb down and wandered off, giving Joanie time to escape. Meanwhile, Joanie had made up her mind. The rough-housing would have to stop.

For the next few days, Joanie remained outside the corral—where she could feed Ruby through the fence and give her water, touch her, talk to her, and just spend time with her. They became friends. Soon Ruby began to look forward to Joanie's daily arrival.

After a while, Joanie went back into the exhibit. As long as Ruby remained gentle, Joanie would touch her and talk with her. But the moment Ruby started to play rough, Joanie would slowly leave. Elephants are social animals; they like having others around. When Joanie left like that, it seemed like a punishment to Ruby. The young elephant quickly learned that if she wanted her friend to stay, she had to be gentle.

Joanie recognized that Ruby was lonely. She knew Ruby craved companionship

Joanie Stinson was Ruby's first real friend.

and had already learned little ways to get it. For example, at night, after Joanie and the other keepers had gone home, Ruby found a way to get the security guard's attention. When she heard the guard making his rounds in his pickup truck, Ruby would toss one of her favorite toys, an old tire, over the rail into the roadway. The guard would get out, bring it back to her, and spend a few minutes talking with her and patting her on the head. It became their nightly game.

Ruby and Joanie entered each other's lives, it seems, exactly when each needed the other. Ruby needed friendship and discipline. Joanie needed the responsibility of taking care of a living creature.

For Joanie, there was another, more personal reason that an elephant became her best friend. Since childhood, she had had a reading disorder called dyslexia. Her brain often scrambled letters and words, making it hard for her to read or write. All through childhood she struggled to recognize even simple words. Children teased her because her spelling was awful. As a result, she became shy and didn't trust many people.

After work at the zoo, Joanie would go home, clean up, and have something to eat. Then she would drive back to the zoo—back to her best friend. She would park her car by the outside fence near Ruby's exhibit, and spend a few more hours at night, talking to her through the fence.

Joanie soon realized she needed help with Ruby. First, she went to more experienced keepers at the zoo. They offered what help they could, but none of them had worked much with elephants. She discovered she would have to reach out even farther. Her dyslexia made written communication difficult and frustrating. But Joanie wanted to help Ruby, and to do so she would have to learn everything she could about elephants. In time, she worked up the courage to go to the nearby university library. Even more frightening, she wrote letters to experts and asked their advice.

Joanie soon made two important discoveries. First, Ruby needed more space. She was growing quickly and would soon be too large for her present home. Zoo officials agreed it was time to build a bigger, better exhibit. But that would be very expensive. It would take years to earn the money.

Second, as Joanie visited other zoos that had elephants, she realized Ruby needed basic training. Basic training for elephants is a lot like obedience training for dogs. It teaches the animals to trust their handlers completely. The major difference is the elephant's size. If an elephant doesn't trust and respect its handlers, their lives are in danger—and the elephant could be in danger too. An untrained elephant will not let a veterinarian treat it. If it gets sick or injured, even minor problems can become major health risks.

To help Joanie and Ruby, the zoo brought in an expert. Franz Tisch was then the elephant trainer at the San Diego Wild Animal Park. In early 1978 he came to Phoenix for two weeks and put Joanie and five-year-old Ruby through basic training. Franz taught Joanie how to stand near Ruby and give commands in a firm, clear voice. It isn't necessary to shout, she learned. Like people, elephants respond to tone of voice. Ruby had a few difficult moments—after all, this was new to her—but basically she was eager to please.

In some places in the world, elephant training is harsh. But meanness and cruelty never pay off in the long run. Franz Tisch had learned to work with elephants in European circuses, where trainers emphasized rewarding good behavior. He was never cruel. He spoke softly.

He won Ruby's confidence by his very demeanor. As someone who had devoted his whole life to elephants, he carried himself with confidence and authority. Ruby sensed this as soon as he entered her exhibit. She accepted him as the boss.

Joanie learned much simply by watching Franz. Still, the training didn't always go smoothly. One day Franz was teaching Joanie how to fasten safety chains on Ruby's leg. She was just finishing when Ruby, like a child having a tantrum, swung her head and knocked her apprentice keeper over backward into a slimy puddle.

Joanie scrambled to her feet, wide-eyed and shaken.

Franz took Joanie for a walk, speaking gently and patiently, calming her, rebuilding her self-confidence. Twenty minutes later, they returned to the elephant enclosure. Joanie entered and gave Ruby the commands to go to the corner and stand still. Then she bent near Ruby's right front leg, wrapped the chain around it, and snapped it locked. She straightened, patted Ruby gently, told her she was a good girl, and gave her a treat.

That moment was graduation: for Joanie, who had just become an elephant trainer, and for Ruby, who learned that being gentle pleased her best friend.

Franz Tisch takes Joanie for a walk to bolster her self-confidence. Afterward Joanie is able to work with Ruby.

3

Over the months that followed, Joanie carefully obeyed the detailed instructions Franz Tisch had left behind. She found that she and Ruby taught each other. Ruby taught Joanie patience and Joanie taught Ruby manners.

One important thing Ruby learned was to pick up her feet, one at a time, and put them on a special pedestal so that Joanie could check the bottoms. Elephants have big feet, but they are soft and sensitive. Just in walking around, elephants often pick up pebbles that can hurt their feet, even in the wild. In a zoo, keepers check their elephants' feet daily, looking for problems and removing them before they become serious.

Ruby also learned to walk around the exhibit, always in the same position on Joanie's right. This way each would know where the other was. Ruby wouldn't get confused and Joanie wouldn't get stepped on.

Ruby even learned to lie down for daily baths so that Joanie could reach and scrub all parts of Ruby's rapidly growing body. A wild elephant would never lie down in the presence of a human being. But each new task reinforced Ruby's and Joanie's trust in each other.

Meanwhile, the zoo raised the money to build Ruby a much larger exhibit, one big enough for several elephants. While plans were being drawn, Joanie began preparing Ruby for the move—two full years ahead of time!

It wouldn't be easy. The little corral was the only home Ruby had ever known. Small though it was, she felt safe and secure there. Furthermore, elephants are always on the lookout for anything that could hurt them. They are suspicious of anything new.

The first hurdle to jump was convincing Ruby it was safe to leave her exhibit. To do that, Joanie needed to teach her to use walking chains.

Walking chains are short lengths of chain that go around an elephant's feet. They allow it to walk comfortably but will trip it if it tries to run. If an elephant gets frightened, it may panic and run. That could be extremely dangerous for the elephant as well as for people, other animals, and buildings—anything that happened to be in the way. And an elephant can be frightened by something you'd hardly notice—a car horn or a new smell or a piece of paper blowing in the wind. So walking chains are essential.

Joanie had a big job in front of her. In teaching Ruby something new, however, she had a secret weapon. Like many animals, Ruby loves sweet feed, a combination of grain and molasses that is something like granola. Keepers often mix vitamin supplements into it. Joanie used it as a treat for Ruby.

One day Joanie arrived carrying a big rubber bucket full of sweet feed. Ruby was immediately interested. Joanie next brought in the walking chains. Ruby hardly seemed to notice as Joanie fastened them gently to her feet.

For the next few days, that's all they did. Ruby stood there, eating her sweet feed, while Joanie let her wear the chains for five or ten minutes. That way, Ruby learned that the chains were nothing to fear.

As the days went by, Joanie gradually encouraged Ruby to walk around her exhibit for a few minutes with the chains. To Ruby this may have seemed like a new game.

Late one afternoon, after the visitors had left, Joanie introduced a big change. She greeted Ruby and entered the exhibit as usual. She put Ruby's walking chains on her

Ruby learned to enjoy her walks around the zoo.

as usual. Then she opened the gate to the outside world—and set the sweet feed bucket on the ground just inside the gate.

Ruby was thunderstruck!

Finally, after a lot of encouragement from Joanie, Ruby slowly and carefully approached the bucket, gobbled the sweet feed as quickly as she could, then scurried back from that open gate. It was a small triumph for Ruby, who received lots of praise and many pats from Joanie.

The next day the bucket was closer to the gate. A day or two later, it was right in the gate. One day it was all the way outside. Night after night, for months and months, this went on, Joanie moving the bucket a few feet farther down the path each time. There were good days and bad days, but gradually Ruby learned to relax, taking longer and longer walks outside her exhibit.

By September 1980, the new elephant exhibit was completed. It was scheduled to open to the public in October. Ruby and Joanie were working their way, still slowly and carefully, down the path to it. A week later, they were exploring inside the huge exhibit yard itself, trying out the wading pool and the dust bath.

A week after that, Ruby and Joanie were spending most of the day in the new exhibit, returning to the old one only at night. A few days later, Joanie walked Ruby over to her new home for good.

Yet, in October, after two weeks of rehearsing several times a day, Joanie still was concerned. She didn't know how Ruby would react to the crowd that was sure to be there on the day the zoo dedicated her new home.

When that day arrived, nearly two hundred guests and visitors came to see the new exhibit and meet Ruby. Once again, however, the rubber bucket filled with sweet feed worked. Ruby and Joanie marched up to it fearlessly. During the speeches, Ruby munched away. When the time came, Ruby raised her trunk in salute, then calmly accompanied her keeper back to the barn for a brief open house.

It was a proud day for a lot of people, but proudest of them all was a shy young keeper who, hidden from view by her prize pupil, allowed herself a big secret grin. They had reached their goal one step at a time.

Ruby salutes the guests on opening day of her new exhibit.

Ruby and Joanie in the new exhibit.

4

Life in her new home was better for Ruby. She had plenty of room to explore, a wading pool, a dust bath, and logs to push around. It was an ideal setting, one in which she and Joanie continued to learn together.

Joanie emphasized firmness, fairness, and kindness. Ruby learned to pick up logs, carry them, and put them down exactly where Joanie pointed. She also learned left from right, front from back, clockwise from counterclockwise. Ruby enjoyed learning new things—and moving the logs around was good exercise for a growing elephant.

Ruby and Joanie weren't learning alone, though. A month after the move, the zoo brought Ruby a companion, a four-year-old female African elephant named Juma.

Juma arrived along with a two-year-old male African named Yati. Joanie was concerned about how Ruby would take to the youngsters. Would she be friendly to them or would she be jealous and mean?

For the first few weeks, Juma and Yati were kept in the barn to give them a chance to get acquainted with each other and to settle down after their trip. Ruby stayed in the yard at night. She enjoyed sleeping outside during the mild Arizona fall.

The day finally came when Joanie arrived at the barn along with several other keepers. She gave Ruby a bucket of sweet feed, then opened the barn door and let Juma and Yati out for the first time.

Introducing elephants to one another is trickier than you might imagine. They don't just shake hands and chat as humans do. They have rules of their own. Elephants communicate through sound, sight, and touch. They make a wide variety of noises, including squeals, grunts, sighs, roars, rumbles, and trumpets. They even make sounds pitched so low that people cannot hear them without the help of machines.

Elephants also signal to one another. A raised tail is a sign of excitement, playfulness, or anger. Fully extended ears on an African elephant can be a warning before a charge.

The trunk plays an important role in communication. Asian elephants greet each other with their trunks. They sniff briefly, identifying one another by smell. African elephants grasp and intertwine trunks. They touch, caress, drape their trunks over one another's heads and backs, and even place the tips of their trunks in each other's mouths.

So how did Ruby react when she met her new roommates?

She took one look and let out the loudest bellow she'd ever made! She ran back about twenty feet, then rushed over to Joanie for protection.

What *were* these strange creatures?

With Joanie beside her, Ruby hesitantly came one step closer, sniffing mightily with her raised trunk and trying to find out who and what these intruders could possibly be.

Juma and Yati calmly walked over toward Joanie and Ruby, their own trunks sampling the exciting new smells. As they got closer to Ruby, she bellowed again and took off in another direction. Yati and Juma followed.

Yati on the day of his arrival.

Juma and Yati.

Ruby hurried back to Joanie. Then she turned and looked—only to find Yati and Juma still following—and took off again.

When Juma and Yati saw Ruby, they must have been delighted to find the first adult elephant they'd seen since they left Africa. They ran to her for protection. But Ruby hadn't seen another elephant since she left Thailand, when she was a baby, so she ran away terrified.

Eventually, Ruby calmed down. Before long she and the infants were smelling and touching and doing all the things elephants do to get acquainted. Within days, they were friends and had formed a herd of their own.

Elephant companions were exactly what Ruby needed. Although there were moments of jealousy when Ruby seemed to resent the attention Joanie gave the youngsters, Ruby and her new friends grew quite attached.

Unfortunately, the adoptive family was not to last. Yati was only a temporary boarder, awaiting a home of his own. That spring, he left for another zoo.

A few months later, in early May, a tragedy occurred.

Juma loved to splash and roll in the wading pool. In doing so, one day she accidentally twisted an intestine and it became kinked. No one knew what had happened. The next day, when she showed signs of illness, the zoo veterinarians gave her medications and tried to help. But it was no use. That night she died.

Ruby took Juma's disappearance hard, and Joanie could not console her. For weeks Ruby wandered the exhibit, searching for her missing friend.

When the story reached the Phoenix newspapers and television, people felt so sad for Ruby that they sent contributions to the zoo to find her a new roommate. The response was so great that the zoo was able to bring two more female African elephants as companions for Ruby.

In June, Joanie and general curator Wayne Homan traveled to a wild animal park in Texas, where they picked out two three-year-old female elephants that had just come from Africa.

Two weeks later, the youngsters arrived by truck in Phoenix. Like Juma and Yati earlier, the infants, named Kewana and Kinte, were kept separate from Ruby for a few days. During that time, they settled down and learned to trust Joanie and accept food from her and her assistants.

Finally, in July, Kewana and Kinte met Ruby. This time, Ruby wasn't frightened at all. Instead, after two months alone, she was overjoyed with the newcomers.

At first there was much sniffing and squirming as all three got acquainted. Then the Africans set out to explore their new home. Repeatedly, straight-tailed with delight, Ruby scurried between the two youngsters. She sniffed them for a long time, then rushed over to where Joanie stood watching as if to tell her about the amazing things she'd just found. Then, unable to contain herself any longer, Ruby hustled over to bang lustily on the metal barn door, making sure the whole world knew how good she felt.

After a sad interlude, Ruby had roommates again.

Juma and Ruby.

In the meantime, someone else had joined the Phoenix Zoo elephant herd. After working in several other jobs at the zoo, Tawny Carlson began as Joanie's assistant in 1981. Tawny was a good student. Her progress over the next few years pleased Joanie for two reasons. First, as Tawny's friend and teacher, Joanie naturally was delighted with her success. Second, Joanie was getting restless. By now she was eager to explore new horizons, but she was also concerned about Ruby and her friends. Luckily Tawny was a natural trainer, and a strong bond was developing between her and the elephants. Joanie knew that if she left, her elephants would be in good hands.

Meanwhile, Ruby, Kewana, and Kinte continued to thrive. Ruby was the leader of the herd because she was larger and older, but Kewana showed promise of someday becoming the leader. She was the one who flared her ears and came forward to investigate newcomers and strange noises.

Finally, in 1985, Joanie left to work at the Brookfield Zoo near Chicago. Although Joanie went elsewhere, she had put her mark on the way Ruby, Kewana, and Kinte

Ruby and Tawny Carlson.

were cared for at the Phoenix Zoo. Besides, the keepers talked to Joanie on the phone regularly, and she came back for frequent visits.

Still, changes were under way. Ruby, now twelve years old, was no longer a cute little calf. Elephant ages are comparable to human ages: at twelve Ruby was about the same as a twelve-year-old person. But Ruby now stood well over six feet tall and weighed close to six thousand pounds—three tons! That's more than fifty times as much as Tawny. And Kewana and Kinte, now six years old, were big and getting bigger all the time.

Elephants aren't the largest animals that ever lived. Several dinosaurs were much larger. The blue whale, a marine mammal, is much bigger. But elephants are by far the largest land animals that walk the earth today.

When Ruby is grown, she may be eighteen feet long and nine feet tall, and weigh up to ten thousand pounds. When Kewana and Kinte grow up, they'll be even larger— up to twenty feet long, ten feet tall, and twelve thousand pounds. That's a hundred times the weight of a 120-pound keeper! And males are even larger.

Because of their size and intelligence, elephants must be treated differently from other animals.

Elephants are wild animals. They are not born tame. You may have seen them doing all sorts of cute things in the circus, but they have the same instincts for survival as elephants that grow up in the wild. You can't just go up to one—not even Ruby— and order it around.

Elephants have their own way of looking at things. In the elephant view of the world, everyone belongs to a herd and has a specific place in it. These herds are actually families—sisters, mothers, daughters, cousins, and their babies. Within the herd, elephants establish a ranking—called a hierarchy—with each animal having a place of its own.

The oldest and most experienced female of the herd becomes the matriarch, the leader and defender. She is the one that knows the way through the forest and across the savanna, where to find food and water, and how to avoid danger. If danger threatens, the adults form a protective circle around the youngsters while the matriarch goes forward to meet the challenge. She decides whether to confront the danger or to signal the herd to retreat.

Membership in herds changes with time. As they grow up, groups of younger females go off and form their own herds. Males, or bulls, are solitary creatures, however. When they reach eight or nine years of age, they become boisterous, and the adult females, called cows, drive them out of the herd. They wander off to live on their own, often traveling a day or two at a time with other males. But elephants can keep in touch over long distances, using sounds so low that people can't hear them.

When Ruby was a baby, she and Joanie formed a herd in which Joanie was the matriarch. When Kewana and Kinte arrived, they joined the herd and took places just below Ruby because they were so much smaller.

When Joanie left, Tawny became the matriarch. New keepers take their places, too, with one important difference. In order to stay alive, keepers *must* establish a rank higher than any of the elephants in the captive herd. If not, amid the constant pushing and shoving, smaller and weaker human beings risk serious injury or death. Elephants kill or injure more keepers than all other zoo animals combined.

Working with elephants is hard and very dangerous. It can take a year or more to earn a place in the herd, even for an experienced keeper.

How does a keeper earn a place at the top of the hierarchy? It begins with the keeper's attitude, as Franz Tisch had shown. To earn respect from elephants, keepers must first give them respect. Respect includes an understanding of how quickly and seriously an elephant can hurt you. But if you're afraid, an elephant will sense it and push you around.

On the other hand, if someone thinks they can bully an elephant, they're in for trouble. No one can make an elephant do anything it doesn't want to do. And if you are mean to an elephant, it will remember. It will wait years for a chance to get even. And when it does, it will have all the advantages.

The keeper's only advantages are knowledge and experience. Keepers must give clear instructions, correct miscues immediately and fairly, and reward elephants with praise, affection, and occasional treats. If a keeper respects an elephant and is firm but fair and kind, the elephant will cooperate.

Ruby and her human herd.

6

Respect for animals also means learning about the care they need. A lot of people have mistaken notions about what animals should eat.

For example, neither Ruby nor any other elephant will thrive on a diet of peanuts. Peanuts are actually a New World plant, so neither African nor Asian elephants would ever eat them in the wild. The tradition of feeding elephants peanuts began in zoos of the nineteenth century. Peanuts were sold as a snack food, and visitors who bought them threw them to the animals. Too many peanuts will make many animals sick, including elephants. That's why most zoos today don't allow visitors to feed the animals.

The proper diet for any animal consists of foods the animal's body needs. For elephants at the Phoenix Zoo, this is about two hundred pounds of alfalfa and Bermuda hay, grain, hay pellets, and various vegetables *per elephant per day!* As the elephants become adults, that amount more than doubles. They also get vitamins and minerals to keep them healthy.

Every other day, Ruby and her roommates get a shampoo.

Proper care also means grooming the animals, much as you might take care of a dog or horse. Elephant skin is very sensitive, so Ruby, Kinte, and Kewana each get a daily bath. Every other day this bath includes a shampoo with livestock soap. The keepers scrub each animal because the elephants cannot scratch themselves on tree trunks and large rocks as elephants do in the wild. The zoo even provides clean dirt so that they can dust themselves. Dust helps protect their skin from insects and sunburn.

The keepers inspect the elephants' toenails and foot pads every day on a sturdy footstool, as we have seen. The elephants also open wide so that the keepers can examine their mouths, teeth, and tusks.

In captivity, elephants depend on people for their health and well-being. They have to be trained to allow human beings

Anita trims calluses.

to treat them so familiarly. The purpose of training is not to teach the elephants tricks. Instead it is to allow keepers and the veterinarian to care for the elephants safely.

The traditional tool in the training of elephants is the ankus. It is a metal hook fastened to a wooden, plastic, or fiberglass handle. The ankus is a keeper's substitute for a trunk and tusks. An elephant's tusks are specialized teeth. They begin to appear when the elephant is about two years old and grow throughout its life. Both African bulls and cows usually have tusks, though not all do. Kewana and Kinte have small but growing tusks.

Asian bulls usually have tusks, although, again, not always. Asian females do not have tusks. Instead, they frequently grow small ivory spikes called tusches.

Most of the time, tusks are used as tools. With its tusks, an elephant can strip bark off a tree or pluck vegetation. Tusks also communicate important messages. Elephants like to be close. Sometimes, however, they get too close, jostling, kicking, and stepping on one another. There's nothing like the sharp point of a tusk to get across the message "Back off!" Finally, tusks are weapons. Bulls may settle quarrels among themselves by sparring and pushing with them.

Keepers use the ankus much as elephants use their tusks—to protect their territory. If a ten-thousand-pound elephant leans on a keeper, a firm poke with a two-pound ankus can save the human being's life.

Mostly keepers use the ankus along with verbal commands to give the elephant a cue. A tap with the ankus near the foot and the command "Foot up!" means the elephant is supposed to lift that foot off the ground. Ruby, Kewana, and Kinte respond to more than sixty verbal commands. Elephants are highly intelligent animals. If a well-trained elephant does something the keeper doesn't want it to do, a firm "No!" will usually put an end to it.

Training itself encourages trust and friendly relations between elephants and keepers. The elephants like the challenge of learning. Since the arrival of their keepers means attention, praise, and treats, training sessions are enjoyable for everyone.

Training and care can be fun for everyone.

7

One spring morning in 1987, Tawny Carlson finished her chores, then carefully locked all the doors to the barn. She climbed aboard her motorized cart, drove up the service road, and turned past the front of the exhibit. As she did, something caught her eye.

"There she goes again!" Tawny thought.

Kewana and Kinte, the two eight-year-old African females, were together, tussling and playing as young elephants usually do.

But off by herself was fourteen-year-old Ruby.

Kewana, Kinte, and Ruby had become friends after five years together, but there was a special bond between the two Africans that Ruby didn't share. The Africans usually ate and slept and explored the exhibit side by side. Ruby wandered in and out of their doings but seemed to spend much of her time by herself. It was what Ruby did at these times that piqued Tawny's curiosity.

Tawny watched, puzzled, as Ruby stood making marks in the dirt with her trunk. She would do it for an hour or so at a time. Sometimes she would pick up a stick or a rock and make the marks with them. But mostly she used her trunk. She'd make a series of marks and then brush them over as if erasing them, or she'd move a few feet and begin another series.

Tawny was intrigued because Ruby's actions clearly weren't merely a random, nervous habit. Instead, Ruby seemed to be making the marks deliberately and studying them intently. Tawny and other keepers had noticed Ruby's behavior even when she was a youngster. She didn't do it all the time. Rather, she did it maybe once or twice a day, in periods like this one, when things were quiet, the Africans were preoccupied, and the keepers were not demanding attention. All in all, it seemed a diversion for Ruby.

"I wonder what it means?" Tawny asked herself. She decided to go to the university library as soon as she could to see whether she could find an explanation. But now she had other animals to take care of and couldn't spend all her time wondering about elephants.

At the library a week or so later, Tawny learned that decades earlier researchers had described how some elephants in the wild would pick up sticks to scratch themselves or to play with. A few also made marks in the dirt—just as Ruby did. But no one seemed to know what to make of it.

In the spring of 1987, Tawny had a brainstorm.

Through the keeper grapevine, she had heard about Carol, an elephant at the San Diego Zoo that had been taught to paint in the late 1960s. At nearly the same time, a friend at another zoo told Tawny that her elephant had dabbled in painting.

Tawny wondered whether Ruby would enjoy painting. One day when she had a little extra time, she gave Ruby an artist's paintbrush.

Ruby took the brush, smelled it, tasted it, and played with it for a while. Then she began to make those same doodles in the sand. She seemed to be drawing in her own way. Tawny gave her lots of praise.

A few days later, Tawny brought Ruby the brush and a piece of cardboard. Ruby quickly learned to direct her attentions to the cardboard. Next Tawny added some nontoxic paint to go with the brush.

It was awkward for Ruby to dip the brush in the tiny jars of paint herself, so Tawny did that for her. Ruby's first paintings were energetic but not very beautiful. She often got more paint on her trunk and Tawny than she did on the cardboard.

But Ruby obviously enjoyed painting. She got excited when she saw Tawny bringing out the brushes and paints. She would waggle her ears, kink up her tail, shake, and make little squeaking noises.

Painting soon became a special part of Ruby's training routine, something she looked forward to. The keepers used it as a reward and invited her to paint when she had done her morning exercises particularly well.

During that same time, painting also helped Ruby adjust to three new keepers. Mike Richardson came to Phoenix from the St. Louis Zoo, Anita Schanberger from the Burnet Park Zoo in Syracuse, New York, and Jerry Brown from the Grand Isle Heritage Zoo in Grand Island, Nebraska. Under Tawny's guidance, each helped Ruby in her painting routine, and she accepted them more quickly than she might have otherwise.

At first, one of the new keepers would hold the canvas while Ruby painted. But one day, Mike was holding a canvas when she went straight up with a brushstroke and painted a blue streak all over him! That night in his home workshop, he made her a three-foot-high adjustable wooden easel for her painting. Ruby enjoyed her painting no less, and the keepers' uniforms stayed cleaner.

Over the next two years, the keepers chipped in out of their own pockets to buy Ruby's art supplies as she progressed from cardboard sheets to genuine artist's canvases. She also learned to use brushes of different sizes and a palette with nine colors.

Ruby's painting soon raised some puzzling questions. For one thing, she seemed to make definite color choices. With her trunk, she would touch a specific jar of paint on the palette. If the keepers dipped the brush in any other color, she would either refuse the brush or drop it in the dirt.

Painting became a special part of Ruby's training routine.

Ruby seemed to have specific color preferences.

The keepers were surprised by this. Do elephants see in color? There was nothing in the books about color perception among elephants. Ruby also had a strong preference for certain colors: red, blue, and yellow. Were these real preferences or was Ruby merely pointing to colors at random? To find out, the helpers switched the position of the jars on the palette and offered more jars. They discovered that, regardless of position and other choices, Ruby continued to choose red, blue, and yellow most often.

The keepers also noticed that Ruby often used colors that matched objects around her—construction vehicles working nearby and even the clothes worn by visitors to the elephant barn.

In November 1989, the keepers had set up the easel for Ruby near the front of the exhibit when a man collapsed near the guardrail. Tawny rushed to the phone and dialed 911. Within minutes the paramedics in their blue uniforms arrived in a red fire truck with yellow and orange flashing lights. Fortunately, the visitor had merely fainted and quickly recovered. Before long the paramedics and the fire truck had gone.

Ruby's Fire Truck

When Ruby and the keepers turned back to the easel, the first color she chose was fire-engine red. The next were yellow and orange like the emergency lights. Finally, she chose turquoise, the color closest to blue on the palette that day. Startled by the painting, the keepers named it *Fire Truck*.

Was it a coincidence or was there another explanation?

That was a tough question to answer. It's one thing for a proud keeper to brag about Ruby. It's another thing to declare positively that an elephant can tell one color from another.

If the paintings were coincidences, another startling one took place right after Christmas Day 1990. On December 28, Mike Richardson brought his four-year-old daughter, Katie, to the elephant exhibit to meet Ruby and watch her do a painting.

Katie was wearing a Christmas present, a sweater that was yellow, pink, and baby blue.

Once Mike introduced Katie to Ruby and the African elephants, Ruby went to work. The colors she chose were yellow, pink, and baby blue—the same colors as Katie's sweater!

Anita Schanberger was especially intrigued. She had studied zoology in college and intended to pursue her studies at the zoo. She wanted to find out for certain whether elephants can see in color. She contacted people doing research on elephants, color, and vision at zoos and universities around the nation. A number of them had wondered about the problem, but few had actually worked on it. The field was open to her.

Katie's sweater and Ruby's painting!

8

Do elephants see in color?

For years people thought that only human beings have color vision. But in recent decades, scientists have discovered that fish, birds, and even insects use color to locate food and avoid danger. But what about elephants? Anita Schanberger soon discovered that the question is far more complicated than you might expect.

How do you find out whether elephants see in color? With human beings, it's fairly easy. You ask them. You show them different colors and ask them to pick one that matches the sample.

But what about animals? Animals don't speak English or any other human language. People don't speak elephant or tuna or lizard. How can we possibly understand animals better? Since they can't talk to us in words, the alternative is to observe them closely and draw conclusions from their behavior.

But that brings up a new set of problems. How do you design a test for a creature you can't talk with? How do you make sure the test asks the question you want answered?

Using the suggestions of her fellow keepers, Anita Schanberger designed a test she hoped would work. The keepers taught Ruby to select an object that matched a color sample they showed her. Initially, they worked with red, blue, yellow, black, and white cones. On command, Ruby would pick up the correct cone when the keeper showed her a card of the same color and called out its name. When she did, Ruby received praise and a treat. Ruby became very good at this. Before long, she could pick the right cone when the keepers simply showed her the color sample. Next, the keepers substituted different objects—balls, cones, cubes, even toys.

But the keepers realized there was a problem with the test. Was Ruby actually making her choices on the basis of color? When photographed on black-and-white film, the cones, balls, and cubes were easily distinguishable by tone. So if Ruby could see only in black and white, she could still do well on this test.

How then do you test for color without unintentionally confusing *color* with *tone*? Certain shades of green and red, photographed with black-and-white film, appear to be middle gray. Thus, their tone is the same even though their color is different.

The keepers made up more tests that they tried with Ruby, but each had some kind of flaw. In addition, the keepers realized they had other problems. What if elephants can see only *some* of the colors human beings see? What if some elephants, like some human beings, are color-blind?

The keepers also learned that the human eye does not see all the colors in the spectrum. There are colors other animals see that we don't. Ruby might not see all the colors we can. But maybe she can see some we cannot!

As Anita got acquainted with researchers around the country, she discovered that some of these problems had already been solved. Tests for human beings had been developed for a long time. Many had been adapted for use with other animals, mostly monkeys and apes. Color testing procedures use special color samples. Numerous colors are available in precise gradations of tone, from bright to dark. By first showing Ruby a sample that matched only one of two tones—a gray and a lighter or darker gray, for instance—a tester could find out how well she could tell one tone from another. Next, by having her choose between different colors—say, a red and a blue—to match the sample shown her, they could prove that she saw color.

In the meantime, Anita, Tawny, Jerry, and Mike set out to teach Ruby how to take a test—one in which there were no wrong answers.

They set it up as a game. Tawny's dad built them a wooden panel with three small windows, one at the top and two side by side a little below it. Into each window, a keeper would insert a card. In the top window, Ruby could see the cue card, printed with a simple shape in solid black: a dot, a square, a triangle, a heart, or a shamrock. The two bottom windows were for the answer cards, only one of which matched the cue card. It was Ruby's job to pick the match.

One keeper would sit behind the panel and move the test cards out of Ruby's sight. The sample window opened first to show Ruby the cue card; then the two bottom windows opened.

Ruby then would grasp a lever under the window of her choice with her trunk. When she made the match, she got a reward—a piece of fruit, lavish praise, and affectionate pats. But if Ruby didn't make the match, the keepers would say and do nothing: Ruby would try again until she got it right. Most of the time, though, Ruby got it right the first time. Kewana and Kinte got their turns as well. After all, the purpose of the game was to encourage Ruby and her companions to enjoy taking such tests.

In the meantime, the keepers continued with their daily work, cleaning, feeding, and caring for all their animals, not just the elephants. From the beginning, the keepers had time for the color studies only when they had finished all their other chores. Often there isn't time left over in the day for more than a few minutes of testing. That's why the search for the perfect test to find out whether elephants can see colors may take years.

What if Ruby can't see in color?

There's no loss at all! The keepers have learned much more about their elephants because of Ruby's painting and because of the testing game. Ruby obviously enjoys the activities. More important, the

Ruby takes a test.

Researchers are continually discovering more fascinating things about elephants.

elephants and keepers have deepened the bond between them by working together so much.

But what if elephants *do* see colors?

Once again we would see how human beings have underestimated elephants and many other kinds of animals. In fact, we are just beginning to discover that many animals have abilities we never imagined.

Recently, one of the Phoenix Zoo's maintenance workers built a steel xylophone in the elephant exhibit. Ruby is fascinated with it and bangs it with rocks and sticks—often when the keepers aren't around.

What if both sound and color are far more important to elephants than we ever suspected?

It may change the way zoos take care of elephants. If elephants are sensitive to color, maybe zoos need to provide more colorful and stimulating surroundings for them. Perhaps keepers have been overlooking important dimensions in their care. Maybe elephant exhibits of the future will be full of colorful furniture—balls, logs, drums, and the like—to keep the elephants stimulated and active. In general, though, the most important result of the experiments with elephants is deepening our respect for them.

9

For the first two and a half years that Ruby painted, hardly anyone outside the zoo knew about it. Painting was meant simply as fun. It was never intended to entertain visitors or to attract publicity. If Ruby were to lose interest in painting, the whole matter would be dropped.

But from the beginning, people who happened to hear about Ruby's painting wanted to see it. And those lucky few who saw her do it wanted to buy the paintings. This raised a question for the zoo managers. Would it be fair to Ruby to sell her work? After much debate, they decided against it. Ruby should continue painting as long as she enjoys it, they decided, but this is a zoo and we take care of animals. We are not in the art business.

In time, Ruby's story got out anyway. Eventually it reached *National Geographic* photographer Bill Thompson, who brought things to a head when he visited in December 1989. At sunset on his last day in Phoenix, Bill Thompson, Tawny, Anita, Jerry, and Mike were standing in the barn talking and watching Ruby and Kewana and Kinte.

The subject of the zoo's decision not to sell Ruby's paintings came up.

Bill Thompson loves elephants. He has photographed them around the world. He has seen the poaching and the destruction of wild elephant homes that are driving elephants—both African and Asian—nearer extinction. Because of this, Bill Thompson is more concerned with the survival of elephants than he is with arguing about whether or not zoos should exploit animals.

"There isn't time for arguments!" he declared. "Don't you realize elephants will be gone from the wild in another twenty years? The only hope for them will be in captivity. Sell the paintings and use the money to benefit the elephants. Build a breeding facility."

An awful silence followed. For a moment the keepers imagined that Ruby and Kewana and Kinte were the last of their species. The sadness was unspeakable.

Bill Thompson's urging also persuaded the zoo administration. Weeks earlier, the Phoenix Zoo Conservation Fund had been established to sponsor projects for endangered species. Now Ruby could both give to the fund and benefit from it.

At the same time, Bill and Gail Bishop, owners of the Bishop Gallery in Scottsdale, Arizona, made an offer the zoo couldn't refuse: they'd host Ruby's world premiere art show and turn over all the proceeds to the Conservation Fund.

All the local television, radio, and newspaper reporters came to the show, which opened in April 1990 with thirty-nine Ruby originals. All the paintings sold in three days!

The story took on a life of its own. Magazines, newspapers, television networks from all over did stories on this

Ruby was becoming a celebrity.

amazing elephant. When Bil Gilbert did an article in the December 1990 *Smithsonian* magazine, calls and letters came from every state in the United States and from five of the seven continents. They came from writers and readers and editors, from television producers and radio talk show hosts, from animal lovers of all ages and accents. Many came from kids.

Most of Ruby's new friends were moved by the compassion that had led to this project in the first place. Many also found the paintings themselves beautiful. Joseph Adano, a professor of art history from Southern California, said he'd been teaching for over twenty years that man was the only animal that could make pictures and that art, therefore, was something only human beings could create.

"Ruby has thrown all that into a cocked hat," he said. "She's forcing us to rethink those assumptions. It's the most exciting thing that has happened in this field in years."

Meanwhile, Ruby's résumé is five pages long, single-spaced, listing interviews and articles, radio and television appearances. A showing of her paintings at the Arizona State University Art Museum in 1991 broke attendance records and was extended four weeks to meet the demand.

As one person observed, Ruby has become the largest figure in Southwest art!

O n television and radio, in magazines, newspapers, and books, Ruby's story—
the story of a lonely elephant calf that grew up to become an international
celebrity—continues to spread around the world and touch people's lives.
It has been told in Bangkok, Thailand, the nation of her birth, and in Rangoon, Myan-
mar, the country next door. It has been told in Brazil, in India, in Russia, and in many
other countries.

And, of course, it has been told throughout the United States. Ruby's story—a
story of hope and dedication, love and friendship—has made a difference in people's
lives.

At a hospital in Oregon, nursing students are learning about Ruby as an example
of what patience and perseverance can achieve. These students will one day work with
patients who have suffered brain damage and must learn over again how to walk, talk,
and take care of themselves.

In an inner-city elementary school in Louisville, Kentucky, a teacher is telling her
pupils about Ruby as an introduction to nature studies.

Tawny and Anita show Ruby paintings sent to her by children all over America.

"These are kids who've never had the chance to see a cow standing in a pasture," she says. "But pictures of Ruby awaken in them an interest in living things. And the story of how she conquered her early troubles gives them hope that they, too, can deal with their problems one step at a time."

In a small town in Arkansas, a family counselor is telling clients, including abused children, about Ruby.

"Ruby's story appeals to children and adults alike. The moral I draw is that, as Ruby and her keepers have shown, patience and kindness can get you through hard times."

How is Ruby herself handling stardom?

Very well indeed. For one thing, the keepers and zoo officials are shielding her from public pressures. Even though the demand for her paintings is enormous—the waiting list was stopped at four years—zoo officials refuse to make Ruby paint any more than she wants. The idea is for Ruby to have fun, not a painting career.

From time to time the keepers offer Kewana and Kinte the chance to paint, but so far neither has shown the interest Ruby has. It's probably their different personalities. Kinte is best at lifting logs and carrying them around. She does that better than the other two. Kewana likes standing on things and balancing. It seems that elephants—like people—each have their own unique abilities, their own talents.

Ruby is the painter. She is the one that made marks in the sand—and still does. She's the one that is teaching us to think again about elephants. How many more secrets lie wrapped up in elephants' enormous hearts—just out of reach until we learn to ask the right questions?

Ruby still paints about once a week. She still waggles her ears at the sight of the paints, the easel, and the empty canvas, and she still kinks up her tail and makes those strange little mousey squeaks.

And millions of people around the world, captivated by the idea of an elephant that makes beautiful images, are discovering yet one more reason to preserve the ultimate animal right: the right to existence.

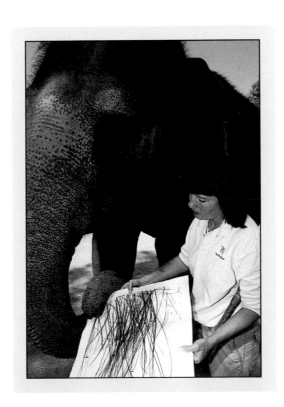

INDEX